INVISIBLE DAUGHTER

INVISIBLE DAUGHTER

JOHN COLBURN

*firth*FORTH
Books

*firth*FORTH *Books*

An Imprint of Queen's Ferry Press
8240 Preston Road
Suite 125-151
Plano, TX 75024
www.queensferrypress.com/firthforth

The characters and events in this book are fictitious. Any similarity to real persons, living or dead, is entirely coincidental and not intended by the author.

Copyright © 2013 by John Colburn

All rights reserved, except for brief quotations in critical articles or reviews. No part of this book may be reproduced in any manner without prior permission from the publisher.

Published 2013 by *firthFORTH Books*

Cover art by Nick Howard

First edition March 2013

ISBN 978-1-938466-16-8

Printed in the United States of America

acknowledgments

Gratefulness to the editors of the following journals, where portions of this manuscript have previously appeared: *Altered Scale, Another Chicago Magazine, Sidebrow, This Spectral Evidence.*

The writing of *Invisible Daughter* was aided by generous grants from The McKnight Foundation, The Jerome Foundation, and The Surdna Foundation.

An enchanted thank you to Sarah Fox, without whose love and support there would be no book at all. Thanks also to Joanna Rawson and Maureen Aitken, who gave valuable feedback along the way, to Nick Howard for his inspiration and generosity, and to Nora Wynn for teaching me so much about daughters.

praise for *Invisible Daughter*:

"A fresh, inspired, and deeply imagined poetic revery on the nature of mutability, family, mythmaking and identity. The limitations of self are upended and explored, as is the nature of place: *Our town went faster and faster, then it left the ground*; of time: *Our trap was time and it could trap anything*; and, above all, the ways in which we perceive and receive the world around us, its terrors and beauties: *We heard the hum of night approach with its moonlight*."

—Rikki Ducornet, author of *Netsuke*

"What an unsettling and gently self-contained world this book is. I love how it patiently explores the different ways it wants to be beautiful and then creates those ways, like a child whose paint set is endless, or an *ashblown spirit* with its own feelings, matters, and events to attend. Built on good colloquial vision, good music, and what seems like well-earned ancestral regard, I love the sense the reader has of being frequently conceived in the book. And how persistent, trustworthy, and warmly catalytic that sense is throughout. When did this happen? You couldn't say for you're alive in the mind now seeking the *Invisible Daughter*. Her whereabouts are complicated, perpetual, and ominous in that way the future seems ominous to the past."

—Peter Richards, author of *Helsinki*

this book is for Jordan Roeder

In The Village Of My Ancestors

Someone embraces me
Someone looks at me with the eyes of a wolf
Someone takes off his hat
So I can see him better

Everyone asks me
Do you know how I'm related to you

Unknown old men and women
Appropriate the names
Of young men and women from my memory

I ask one of them
Tell me for God's sake
Is George the Wolf still living

That's me he answers
With a voice from the next world

I touch his cheek with my hand
And beg him with my eyes
To tell me if I'm living too

—Vasko Popa

Mantorville, Minnesota, 1979

I. brotherhood

*I'm in the dark on a long long long lonesome road
a roadless road . . .*

—John Taggart

story

We pretended to die in backyards. Birds waved their songs at us. The woods grew along our creek at the edge of town. A lucky voice asked why. On the town side, up the hill, the metal shop glimmered and people there went deaf. Outside the shop Fat Dewey told this story: *Once there was a father who left his daughter and walked into the forest. In fact, that forest there. When he had walked for three days, a flickering vision of the daughter appeared to him. She was sad of heart from head to foot, but she allowed the father to walk with her and hold her hand for a time. Then his hand suddenly felt cold, and when he looked at her she vanished. The father found himself alone in the woods and very tired. He lay down beneath an oak tree. As he slept, winter came. His breathing slowed, his hair grew thick. He hibernated, like a bear. When he woke it was spring, he had acorns growing in his hair. He thought that everything was a dream so he kept trying to wake up. He's still out there, trees growing from his head, waking up over and over, every spring. His invisible daughter is out there too. That's all I remember.* Dewey spat. From the shop we watched each leaf. Some stones turned to butter in the sun. We said let's look for the daughter. Find her.

welcome

We didn't know our town happened in a nest of spirits, in the dark, full of noise. Let me guide you: Our town smelled of insects. People's legs could not bear heavy talk, we slept, we stayed home. We drank the stories and ate the stories every minute. Science told us to worry about the future. There was a law. Our town flamed in valley darkness then puffed out, a balloon town. We imitated toy animals, leapt in close bedrooms. Not much was known of us bright brothers, grass thick, of surprise doors rising in the hills. How we shrunk the flickering spirits with our pale light. Our town vanished down a long dead road. Inside the woods a voice called away. We might fail at civilization but still, welcome to the cloudy dream made by ancestors. The streets seemed unfinishable. Were we in somebody's reflection, and did our porch lights shine back to the other side. We found unknown light and built a road over it. We circled the house three times to shelter ourselves from blight. Sidewalks warped and became slippery. What dream, what dream. We found our jobs. We kept moving.

work

Our job was to find spirits in the woods. They became lost inside themselves or lost inside an argument, they wandered hills in a state of detachment. We found them and told them to get out of bed. We said *Build a tendril.* Or we shined light into them and if they were blinded, we could be blind with them, swim out toward a sound or a name, a piece of paper, even slip into their dreams, pull them toward the dull life in everyone's rooms and say *Please, understand this map, it's blank, you are here,* and sometimes the spirits were ourselves. We met and decided to be brothers. We found trees that spoke in our foreheads and we touched any dead beasts. We blessed fallen-out teeth. A forest created itself. We napped in the ripening south. Strangers lost their way, dew formed on the path. The road wouldn't stop. We were finders.

talk

No one worshipped the creek. Our town mined the bluffs. The schools grew sturdy. Take this stone into the woods. Take this apparition to the corn and soybeans. Older Brother said *What will you say when you meet her?* I said *I'll whisper something.* Our town resembled flies and birds at dusk, hovering above boxes of seed. Our town drank sleep and paid no attention. We listened to darkness spread over windows. Stood at woods-edge with our weary story. Older Brother said *You go first*, to break the cobwebs. I said *No you.* We closed our eyes and saw branches. I thought *I'm sorry there's a downstream.* We built a limestone shrine. We hid the flashlight. A crow hopped by the creek, looking in.

thursday june 14 1979

We ran the feral beginnings of town, old stagecoach road through the woods, memory of horses straining along the ridge. Invisible Daughter bent at the creek, believing with her wolf bucket and we ranged from tree to tree, blind in ropey grunts. She made a past and a future with stones in a wet bucket, daughter growing dimmer in the valley, sound rose from the green fast water and the name of the woods grew. Finders heard the wooded hiss. Finders saw the sleep in you. We watched how lost sounds became blue in loud light at dusk. We strained along the ridge. No sound now but the sound of smoke. Is it horse or is it happiness? Silence slipped behind our noise. No sound now but the sound of smoke.

search

We really wanted a few rich people to suffer. We really wanted unconscious burning against the pillow. We really wanted to loosen our history from under the creek, to act like a tent and do it in secret, to be classified as a thing in total oblivion. We really wanted primordial homework, to write *forget* down the page over and over without consciousness. We wanted another night, then another night, all our equipment in one hand and hidden in our creep toward dawn, still another night. We really wanted a white bed in the woods for one hour, we really wanted comfort.

methods

One way of searching the woods began in a room, alone, in lungs and ears, because daydreams made fantastic history, made ridges upright in the steaming body. One way resembled condensation, sudden appearance, memory forced from the body by bird, leaf or glass, by the creek, by inventing ashes or discovering them, we were never sure. Many animals jumped out of our shrine. We just put them back word by word. Rain could make a temple. One way was convulsive. One we called punch-and-run: search the sleepers, punch the dream and run. One way was tied to the animals' foreheads and we followed them in.

friday june 15 1979

I fell into trance. Animals appeared and disappeared, we flew over the old stagecoach road then we were hair being combed, then wrapped in dreams. I saw a green bat, a black deer, a wild boar thickening in the rain. The trance lasted all night, a flower grew from human bone, all night ended, the sound of one small bird telling a story, turning to snow, careening along the shoulder, sound of what comes next, glass going out into the night and I wanted the trance, I missed the silence it contained, all the animals, my parents, the constellations glittering over our front porches, their songs pressing us blind, and I woke in the ditch at the ungraceful bottom of myself, one leg bent backward, owned by the county, I woke awash and mangled in the lilies.

story II

The shop pulsed with sound. We asked Fat Dewey for more. He said *Someone gave the daughter a terrible flower, it never opened, it had the potential to become human, it was special. The mother knew the someone must have been a man. That's all I remember. There's something about a stagecoach driver who ate his horse once in a blizzard. But that's different.* Sand dunes, baldness, sunset, butterflies. Everything moved. Fat Dewey walked the long hill down to the creek and fished a can of beer from his hiding place. We spied. The town grew solemn. In the woods pages of light folded. Snakes finished sunning themselves and slid home. We wanted to teach Invisible Daughter to be solid. From head to foot.

cold cold

Take this stone into the woods. We weren't brothers. Then we were. In shadows of pine trees, touch the cold ground at dusk and feel waiting. Into the woods there came a daughter, she was given a terrible flower. At the creek where future daughters whirled we looked for gold-reflecting people or we unraveled feathers arced toward ruin in cold fallen earth with marbled fruit or was cold just the future and how cold would it be not under but in-ground and backboned with sapling voices running up mirrored hollows. The waiting cold was possibly a giant and the creek was alive, water lived. We tried to kill the water with flat, heavy rocks. We threw them down from the sky. How it could all grow out of cold. We waited. A frosted bird climbed. For everyone and their grape jelly.

saturday june 16 1979

We looked through trees for three days. We sat still and waited for her to find us. We threw more rocks. The creek talked in chorus, dream to dream. I landed on an idea, a way. Stones scuttled behind grass. We walked through the summer of not thinking. We searched the woods for blood in a gust of wind, for speech, for a father's strange words, for horses grown from earth in a single wave. Then we found her. Stones made butter. One ghost was enough. The moon played wolf. We dined on reflections in the lowland because finders got feelings from dreams and followed them in. A still space turned and touched down. We found her.

invisible daughter

Truly we stole beer and ran into the woods. A substance formed. The beer tasted like wood rotting in water. We danced around. Our ceremony narrowed. Guests arrived from the eighteenth century. Summer formed a fist. *Look out, do something.* Our tissue unwound. Below us the cold creek turned. In the chill we felt her thistle. She was asleep. Her sleep made the forest deeper. Her god was empty. She took the form of a cold spot at a bend in the creek, a reflection hovering at the rapids, a voice weaving green sparks to the creek bank. She saw us, she flickered, her face traveled in waves and her pale rooty throat swallowed my future sleep, my quiet. She saw two warm strangers in modern underwear. I said *How-do*. Older Brother threw a rock at the creek. Ripple. She disappeared.

landscape

The creek went still. Don't get sick. We floated dry husks down. Our question: *When does now end?* We looked for lights inside birds. The creek managed us with its sly force. We saw the trees and vines and fruits and grasses as they faced us then looked away, saw leaves we would always love falling in the night as we slept in our shivering monastery and knew the houses would capsize and the money would burn and we imagined deep jungle roses taking a person's life and stone skulls working up through earth, we were late for dinner, the spirits shook their gongs, we were finders. A stone noticed me. A frog's red mouth. Outside the woods we were unimportant.

report

Fat Dewey, we saw Invisible Daughter, down through water with a face like a bell and she is cold, she needs a blanket, she turns invisible, she talks through water and wet leaves, her nose is white, it's when you feel a chill, she's there, we saw her kneeprints in grass by the creek, we saw her reflection, life hangs on but there's no summer for ghosts. Fat Dewey said *Why aren't you looking for the father? He can't even go invisible.* That's why! That's why! Our looking surprised the woods. Maybe we increased the spirits. Maybe an insect dried up right there and lost its soul. Maybe a dangerous spirit, shaken out of a robin or blackbird, fell into us.

dream

I tried to talk. Invisible Daughter blurred my dream. I became a radio or an opera house ghost. Many figures appeared but could not hold form. A red snake slept in my shoelaces. I carefully unwound him. I saw everyone who lived in our town, then everything they imagined, dim and superimposed. Even a horse made from the eleven divine powers. I couldn't see Invisible Daughter when I looked at her. Was I in the father's dream? She appeared as an influence, a form on the periphery, a green glow. What is an aura? I followed the snake as it made history. This stone was touched by a stagecoach horse. This one escaped from a body. This one had holiness. Was I the father's dream? How do you know what you already know but can't? Some snakes burn everything they touch. An aura looked at me and I became its mind. I heard the red cartoon snake sliding along and it sounded like rain, like the color red, singing.

II. exchange

I am carried in my shadow
like a violin
in its black case

—*Tomas Tranströmer*

the past

We put our ears on limestone fossils to hear the ocean floor. Speech had gotten stuck in our big steak dinner. Our town could dream. The creek stretched out a long name. Each fossil carried a shout of joy, a mind to feel hungry with, enough thought to understand stars. All bleached. All the dogs in town pointed their music at us. We listened. We felt welcomed in the caves, animal forms slow as clouds. Caves that are really caves can dream. Up the ridge earth's wheel got louder. My horse was so tired. How did we go from the ocean floor to the pony express? We climbed. Invisible Daughter helped us. *Sad of heart from head to foot.* The time of stars and ocean streaked through us, we walked like branchless trees. In deep sleep the past appeared dead, we could see it in each other but we couldn't understand. Stars fell backward in great tides. We watched.

tuesday june 19 1979

We knew Invisible Daughter could flicker awake too. Somewhere in the trees moon war guns veils dances love all memory light bent inside light and water voices eyes road hands language all inside trees. We decided to set a trap. What else could flicker? The road flickered with ghosts and hoofbeats. We sat still to watch the edges of leaves. The father slid awake and the mother was everything. We stalked Invisible Daughter through the blackberries. Green leaves could flicker into silver. Shadows moved east. Trees said waves. We needed a wagon to carry what was said through the town. The creek flickered to its underground family. Stars were fires and fire might be a ghost and flickered. No one could turn back ever. Our trap was time and it could trap anything. We built a small fire-in-waiting, altar for a cold ghost girl. Ghost fire. We surrounded the altar with our hoarded baby teeth. Does the woods know the earth is round? Are we inside a bubble? Someone lit the fire. Maybe ghost girl missing a tooth. Then we heard footsteps.

acquaintance

At the edge of our fire a garden of people began to remember themselves. Pilgrims came for teeth, to eat or steal or crush them. One footstep turned red. Invisible Daughter would never. At the edge of our fire we saw Thought-Eating Man as if light were behind him, as if he had walked through a light to come to our light and our teeth and our fear. He had a dead blackbird in his heart. How do you kill a tooth? Older Brother grabbed a stick and it started afire in his hand. We heard the hum of night approach with its moonlight. Thought-Eating Man stepped toward us. There were others our fire made a nest for. Probably hundreds we couldn't see. Eyes raced in the gully. Fangs of light tunneled. Invisible Daughter had friends or enemies. Our town was built inside another town and both were falling apart. We heard Thought-Eating Man shifting off. Footprints of light formed and sank into the leaves. One less tooth, and a shard of fire went green.

definition

Check your dictionary. Check the windblown trees in the flashlight beam. Our town learned to report accidents by telephone. Children stood still when it rained and later were used to haul sleds. Ships began to sail to the cemetery to make butter. No one saved eggs. We invented great nets for receiving letters. We tried to choose our lunches wisely. Maybe electricity could repair the roof. Maybe our pet rabbit made its own settlement. Our town developed its nighttime stomach and stepped out of dreams. Bedtime stories exploded. The amount of eye makeup we used almost killed us. Our town rented mouths. Dusk settled for at least an hour, we took off our clothes for twenty years and there were still more clothes. Our circle lengthened. Our town went faster and faster, then it left the ground.

prophecy

At dusk we found holes in the road and looked through. We found nests. Empty spaces gaped awake inside us. The woods appeared peppered with mouths that spoke light. The creek gave birth to its trees. We looked into the moving empty, the snowy summer doorways, a church spinning its black hole in the last hour. We stomped our fire too late, Made of Ashes walked the woods and heard each leaf's omen. Older Brother said *We will suffer because of Thought-Eating Man.* He couldn't say how. Unreasonable light built up inside me, I was an incomplete child. A death-white shoulder. I was called into the hills to stay lucky. Who was finding who, and with what? A history book, a record player, an elbow. The creek and the fire let our thoughts inhabit them. There was something to say but maybe it was saying us. I cleared my throat: *Are we in the father's dream?* Another hole opened in the road or we had just come through it.

tongues

One word and then another, each more beautiful than the last. We moved forward by saying her name. Inside or with the woods, on the limestone outcroppings, swinging tree to tree down hills, we knew the other side spoke, tongues flickering in waves of forest light. I said *Show me what daughter of what.* Because what if Invisible Daughter was a mirror. What if she was a doorway. What if she was a sky. What if she was an insect. What if she ate our regular eyes and we only saw mirrors. What if she was just grass and wind. What if we only saw into fires. Music from the snake and the frog and all the mouths swirled beneath the ridge. What if spirits pursued us all the way home? Each step thinned our moan. We saw in tongues. Someone bought a Cadillac. Noise from the metal shop echoed in creek water. It acted like a magnet, and we were drawn. *Fat Dewey, Fat Dewey. Fire made a door and we left it open.* We woke up in light or light knocked us into another sleep. We said names. The miracle bubble froze. We feared everything was shadow.

friday june 22 1979

Thought-Eating Man followed us, behind trees. Dewey couldn't see. I said *He's got bright fruit.* Then a man laughed ahead of us, he telephoned the moon. We threw handfuls of rocks on the metal roof and ran toward the woods. Men rushed angrily out, stood outside and decided to smoke. In town, hands down. We recognized a darkness, a dragging footstep. Had we gotten torn down in our dim days and crushed gravel roads? In town we were trouble, in the woods we were hunted. We decided to wade the creek, praying above its path of mirrors. Old days lingered in the water and passed undecided. We heard the bells of town and a far-off chainsaw and wind rustling. No harm would come to us while we were being born.

science

A fat flock of robins pooled at the creek, normal Sunday, haze after sunrise and stones breathed slow, haze from burning bodies and spirits where I walked forgotten in a house of dust and rain and if I didn't dream I woke and pried its closets. We lollygagged in the forest, aware of new ghosts, and knew our portion of the prayer to be silent, just two boys who opened a door. Our trees emerged. We classified new spirits in the name of science. What boundary traveled into the flame? We discovered every moment as it came toward us. Spirits swam past. We called one Owner of the First Embrace, it arched like a scream. We saw the white dog and the black dog together and they said *We seek to haunt* and we called that one Dewey and we laughed. Leaves gave us clues in both worlds. A fat flock gathered a million miles away and how did we know.

memory

From the empty space over the snowdrifts, the long fields absent of sound or spirit through the indoor winter of looking out into nothing, we loved discovering spring and how spirits moved and did they have mouths and what did they do with their hands or what sounds did they make, we loved finding out the woods were alive and we were alive and the town thrummed, and were the spirits able to smile and if so when did they, were they gentle or were they fast, did they play games with us or hate us or need us, how did they react to a joke, what did they look like when asleep, how did they touch each other, how did they eat, did they shiver. I guess someone built a fire in the spring and let them out and they wear looks of great concentration or do they even have looks and can they travel to hell or ride on the wheel of fortune and what is their natural depth and will I get headaches and what do they remember and how do you even ask them a question?

school

I remembered school for an instant, sunlight through ripe sky, room full of reading children, we shake and twitch in a lake of shadows, day one of tennis shoes, we fill with words and now what and now a good distant feeling rings, we are unable to pay attention, one boy who stares out the window, we read a book together, there was a dog, and what did we do last night? The sun changed in the memory, everything difficult to explain like a world of doors or of day ones, unspeakable, the same door again. Again.

meal

Transparent and naked, the spirits ate. Every world hungers and happily works a million grim engines to feed itself. When we walked in the woods outlines appeared. We walked at the edge of ourselves looking into the other nation. Who was reading from pages trapped in our balloon heads? Grains fell into our veils. Spirits ate daydreams and explanations, the vibrations of trees, they hunched in the wind, ate from our happiness and anger until we became plain and they ate like hammers ringing in silence. I walked the stagecoach road and stopped for a spirit. At first it seemed less than a scar in air, then it jellied up. The sound of it sounded in my ears. The spirit said *What will you hear?* and I ran down the hill toward town, afraid of being talked to but also afraid to lose the memory. I sat in a lawn chair in my backyard and wondered if spirits were eating me. All the trees seemed aflame with light and insects and tree talk. Someone drove a ridiculous car past. I tried not to listen.

conversation

In our houses wood glowed and the grain of the bedroom doors showed frozen faces of old spirits. Our whole town sat like a cemetery. I dreamt of horses and a morning god who drifted into each person and disappeared. Late at night I floated in a water mind. Invisible Daughter could only speak to us in dreams. I began to pull wagons in my sleep. I pulled them through the forest and noticed how the sunlight felt older. How an eyelid flowers up from the chest and opens. The old stagecoach road carpeted with stars. Invisible Daughter appeared. She said *You're not very good at making friends.* I asked her to touch ground and she said that was for living things and living things were trapped in god like minnows in a creek. She hovered right there like the moon. I pulled my wagon up the wilted stars. *You are invited to a sleepover,* she said. *At my house.* I told her my wagon was already full of sleep and I had to pull it. *That sleep is dead,* she told me. *Those are memories.* I looked back. She was correct. It was all dead as a sundial in the black night.

parents

Breakfast folded and crept along. I had to ask. In our cemetery tin music hovered. My parents smelled of civilization. A coffee cup sound. *Can I camp overnight in Older Brother's backyard?* Breakfast became a test of breathing. Mom said *He's not your brother.* We looked around at the wind. I had outgrown the word haunted. We ate living things. One parent was polyester and one was cotton. Their pancakes glowed. I must have betrayed them. Dad said *The tent is pretty heavy.* Which meant yes. In sleep my parents slipped home to dark waters, became elders, forgot their baskets of flowers and left the path. Now we made a chord. I saw a spirit in the ceiling, it told me to turn off the radio. My parents found dense words that meant yes. I hoped I didn't become a door right then. A door slows you down.

exits

That woods is filled with exits. It is patrolled by finders. Come the pine trees with their questions. The creek raises its miracle. Pitch a tent in the fruit of the head, may we sleep and remain on earth, may we find bluer water in sleep and pass singing into houses where Original Daughter and Invisible Daughter are one, may we find the knowing beast in full tide, and witches with mirrors and knots of herbs and drumbeats from the far shore, may we call to them at the blue edges of twilight and sunrise and may they hear the drone of people from that country, the lapping at the gate almost like silk, the reverent heart to assist with burning, the scattering of teeth. Fifty paces in a hundred years down a seam of forest. Each exit has a keeper. Exit into the boiling others. Exit into summer rain.

provisions

Wavering speech drifted over the valley buildings. Older Brother wondered should we make a map. We decided there were no maps and we took rope. The tent hung in the garage like a body. We took songs and a touch on the ditchgrass and we took food. We took gills. We took one perfect throwing stone each. We took a knife then left it in silence on the garage floor. The town flooded with sun, shrank, grew strange. It became noble to have six matches each. Our provisions included simple thirst, flashlights and food, untold names assumed in sleep, walkie-talkies with Morse code buttons, the violence of our stories. We stood in the early hush of ourselves. Each thought had its own voice inside, and inside that, and on and on. We walked through his backyard and saw the metal shop glowing, just up the road. All of the woods and all of its worlds and spirits turned their faces around and around and the creek flickered. We smeared milk pods on each other's foreheads and waited to become grooms or fathers and we weren't afraid. Bright sun fired the creek light. We were finders.

III. call

*I walk in the land of many gods,
and they love and eat one another.*

—Linda Hogan

camp

At a shallow spot in the creek we carried over. We knew to stay off old stagecoach road. The fragrant morning going away. Slanted light through our heads. In what language should we make our camp? The tent like a body brought to be released. We made a temporary home on the ledge over the creek. It bothered us to lie. We saw the jaws of a cave on its endless journey through space. Older Brother unrolled the tent. What eaters we would be. What hiders and finders. Time wanted us and would have us. We arranged provisions at the perimeter, flashlight in place, each throwing stone in its cradle, holes for feet and hips. We raised the tent and made another door to another inside, tied white flags on ropes to see in moonlight and to surrender, always to surrender. A camp for murmuring funerals; electric, baited spirits circling continuously and the creek below feeling its stones. We heard footsteps and frying air and vines growing. Invisible Daughter must have talked or sang about us or the father dreamt us down to the woods and dreaming happens at the speed of fire and our childhood might be consumed by spirits listening to our camp right there on the ledge, surrounded by wind and talking and outer space.

preparation

Our bones, blank as windows, suddenly filled with light. Two boys crushed by the thrill of contact. We felt ourselves forming as spirits formed. I imagined a rattlesnake tie, a pit pouring green, the wake of Invisible Daughter as she pulled us along. Older Brother peered over the ledge. I saw a leg on the ridge and I prepared. We pre-built the fire, arranged its teeth. We sang hanging songs. Acorns fell to the skin of the tent while the town, its courtrooms, its mailboxes and slow traffic, tumbled in sun. We made a path to the old stagecoach road and hoped for dark, impatient, we looked up the far hill toward town but it wouldn't go away, I was blond and short, days followed me into the woods and school would find me and teams and girls and parents walking slowly in abandoned hallways, we were bright green and waited to grow blue at dusk and be fed to spirits. I could smell Invisible Daughter rocking back and forth in the breeze, but were we prepared for the great force, were we prepared for the slowness of dark events in the sky. Shape after shape rose from the creek. We watched great banks of gray clouds in fast creation cross our valley.

saturday june 30 1979

We trampled through stands of young trees. We were a danger to the organism. Far off in our shy woods we heard domestic life, a mother settling into evening, squirrels up and down jagged bark. Were we a danger to the organism? We had become a danger. Thought-Eating Man loomed elsewhere, tension pulled the saplings. We practiced walking blind, one one-thousand, two one-thousand. We trained ourselves to sense auras: stop and be still and look askance. Shelter could be sound or smell or a shape wind makes in maples. We tuned our ears to any distant kingdom. Our mouths swelled with hush. We trained the auras onto our t-shirts. Older Brother moved his walkie-talkie atmosphere around. He heard spirits croon the static. At creekside we stacked wet rocks and felt their buried hearts. We built a dam for Invisible Daughter, to see her while she saw herself, a time trap, and the slippery creek grew a slow gray belly, rock after rock. We never thought of cameras. We snuck behind crayfish and they backed into our hands then danced, held to sunset, claws agape. Invisible Daughter was also a finder. We watched the first spotted fawn of dusk, chewing.

fathers

Older Brother's father waved from up the hill on the far side of the creek. We stood on the unnamed ledge, waving beside our bright orange tent. I became afraid more fathers would disappear, fathers from the future. We saw the last daylight spirit cross the creek disguised as a plateau of quiet. In town fathers rose and tramped through dusk behind their lawnmowers. A crow flew through a cold rope of air. Past fathers emerged from mud and started to proclaim; we turned away. Then we were children burning alone in the stumpy woods of some long-ago father's dream, castaways building a transparent city, fizzling in time. We had no ideas but our mouths could laugh. We said goodbye to guiding hands, we dimmed in the wavy, delirious summer, we began to debate. Older Brother said *A spirit can't ever be solid.* Thought-Eating Man made a song somewhere by whistling through grass, so we would know. Finders understand human direction. Everything behind us was flame. The song deepened and disappeared, seemed to say darkness then darkness happened, sky no longer sky but an opening toward a song. We stood wondering for a dumb moment what was to come and the fathers, stunned by time, turned on lamps and opened newspapers and the animals and spirits rustled up from sleeping places to find whatever sustained them, their valley and its night.

surprise

In darkness surprising words appeared in our minds. I felt I needed speech therapy or white hair, I felt seductive and deep. As if I knew where a star might shine. I hoped we could leave time or break the arms of spirits and watch them grow back. I hoped for sleep easing its calm under our tent, dense dreams like pomegranates. Long ago a new part of earth had thickened underwater and now we stood on it. Dinosaurs had dreamt here and left tremors. Maybe tomorrow we would have powers, maybe we would disappear into the woods like ingredients. Older Brother stared into the forming pool. Our blue air turned one shade bluer. Fireflies lit up a natural stairway, creek to ridge, all limestone. We knew the devil never made trees and I touched the vibrating trunks, studied the ridge, a tight waiting entered our dimming camp, a preoccupation. I told Older Brother I saw spirits inflating and delivering their own bodies, it was hard to explain. I told the trees and creek, the crayfish under their rocks, and either it was true or I wanted deliverance from truth. Would I know if I lit up? I thought betrothed, engulfed, saturated, confidential, lapidary. Strange words.

teeth

The way to start is fire. Our noble matches. Baby teeth from little paper envelopes, placed one each on rocks in a circle round the fire. Older Brother turned bluer. I didn't look at the town behind me. We lit the match and stared. A rope moved by itself through the trees. Our spines and necks tightened. Our jaws clenched. A feeling of carbonation. Then, activity in the corners of sight. Odd lights and shapes caught our attention. The fire. Savage tooth fairies! The flame caught and held itself. Our rule was not to add wood. A presence labored toward our circle, like wind that didn't move anything. We sang the chosen John Denver ballad. My own father somewhere, and his father. Our half-moon appeared. The fire made a clock. We grew large or time grew larger. Older Brother became afraid: *What if a spirit exactly my shape stepped into me? No one would know.* The teeth glowed. They had fallen right out of our bodies. I picked up a throwing stone. A dream covered by leaves felt its way toward us. Some of our stars were real. All the possible ways to throw a stone. The fire shrank. Instead of night we had the teeming day inside out.

nightmare

They came through the trees like raindrops. Our fire disappeared and we shone flashlights into the living dark. The crowd of spirits turned and they were the trees, each leaf had a voice, each voice made a needle feeling in our skin, a song of being alive in the woods. Older Brother rippled, he had to pee, he said *What if I pee on a spirit?* Dark figures moved their summer through my chest. One spirit with a hundred faces flashed into view, I didn't know how to look, I wanted a look. Older Brother huddled on the ledge. I came to the creek and bent over its slow dark, its loud going on. The reflections of stagecoach people, dinosaurs, a giant udder, future people torn from the creek, some of them could talk, some could not. We were organs of the woods. I saw outlines like toys scattered on a bedspread. I shouted up *Do you see them?* Small sounds magnified each place. From far into himself, from a future he visited in daydreams, with a voice from the marriages and long workweeks of our fathers, Older Brother said *Worse, they see me.* I closed my eyes but spirits were in my mind place. So much sound and being carries across earth only at night. I was just learning.

meeting

Maybe Older Brother's flashlight and walkie-talkie weren't real. Between us we grew separate heavens. Any doorway must be part fake, a doorway grows into open space. We saw an ashblown spirit flash the air then disappear. Older Brother said *What if that was its whole life?* I was too young for that—a no-entrance thought, don't build it. Too late. I dreamed my shivered flash. *Good evening people inside me.* The woods surged, a complete round tone like a wild plum. Our little fire doorway, our little tooth call. Older Brother wandered downstream with his light and its urge. What was inside him? I saw a raccoon made of fire, green and low and trundling after. Right then I loved my parents' deep, bedded sleep, I loved the sleep of dandelions. And how does the creek sleep. I watched for plants that were faces and trees that were animals, afraid to meet some spirit of myself or the cave silence makes. Was I not born alive? Was the great darkness really water? All doorways around me, I stood still in thousands of sounds. Who was better, who was the best spirit?

thought-eating man

He eats us all then dreams our lives. He has gone wandering through our gods. At the creek I had the feeling of song, of orchestra, of the leaf-covered dream expanding through ages. I saw a shape surface, the time trap at work. Thought-Eating Man stood next to me, looking into himself. His two mouths breathing. He held a hand toward me. I knew not to become adult. Night changed constantly: darker, deeper, now more purple, now more echo, more beyond. Thought-Eating Man wheezed in stereo, an abandoned spirit, a different person every thought. I wanted fresh cool light around my chest. But what if I forgot my thoughts. He clouded or furred, I couldn't tell in darkness. The creek got simple with bugs. What if someone far away were imagining me and that was my life, just a shape. Through-Eating Man tried to give me a language. It was uncomfortable; I knew I was waiting to know. He held my teeth to the moonlight. I crossed over, toward human shapes glistening in the limestone. Thought Eating Man could wait forever. I wanted my mind.

multitude

When you look at stars they spark and disappear, unknown hundreds every look, you close your eyes and stars flare in your eyelids, each tree breathing slow among extravagant sounds of night, you look. Flash. I entered the canopied stairway, vast insides of my little body lit, stars and leaves singular, each an incandescent example, each a gravity enacted. Is now the surrender? It keeps coming, here then there and for a moment, you. Look into grasses and beetles and stars and clouds. No comfort. The trickle of boys through woods in time, god we were being eaten, we were followed all our lives. I wanted up, toward the streaking stars, I climbed, the future and past together just a hill. I saw more shapes. People shapes from different times left the creek and roamed hills like the course of a song. I ran from tree to tree, touching my way uphill. I heard the creek and the town and the moon speak inside me. The spirits of even leaves, even rocks talked. Does there have to be a point to everything a boy does?

invisible daughter II

I walked the ridge alone and stood in a rousing dark on old stagecoach road. Our walkie-talkies crackled. We wanted evidence of inner now. All these animals will kind of die. Older Brother threw a loud rock at the creek, the far-off town spiraled away. Were there unseen navigators? I heard more rock on rock, like bones breaking. There were no birds. Why did Older Brother's mind never wander? It seemed inhuman. I walked on remnants of road. Maybe Older Brother was a spirit. I saw two floating lights then tasted them, sweet and coppery. Maybe something could be not dead and not alive. Just deeper. The moment happened, a form of night taking speech, lights passed through me then Invisible Daughter held my hand. We stood gut still at zero distance. She warmed the woods. Her sudden hand. I wasn't sure I had a mouth to speak from. I pressed the walkie-talkie button but what world was it in. Invisible Daughter said *Thank you.* I waited for my voice. Plus it was night in which world? From the walkie-talkie shrunken Older Brother said *Who was that? Who was it?* A bird or bat swooped through starlight. Invisible Daughter allowed me to walk with her. I held her hand for a time. It suddenly felt cold. When I looked at her she vanished. I felt tired. Walkie-talkie like a big broken ear. Our half-moon lay on its back. Never hide from a daughter.

alone

Coming back from heaven, the ridge was heaven, I walked through a cobweb. The walkie-talkie bleeped Morse code. A spirit washed me. I studied Invisible Daughter as a new memory. I learned walking. I learned floating above fossils. I learned the woods bends to your light when you're being lovely. Invisible Daughter taught gestures learned from plants, she was symbiotic, there's not just one mind in a person. I became a passenger. Her will floated through the woods. I learned, I descended. Our interpreters floated over dark earth. The path seemed lit by my eyes, lit by looking. I saw Older Brother walk toward the tent and said *Are you a spirit?* He said *Don't play. Don't.* Our background changed lights, a mute future shined on. The woods soaked us in its brown and green beard. Another spirit, Made of Ashes, poked at the cold fire. The best way to get rid of a ghost is to become one yourself. That works for dictators too. Maybe fathers. A finding spirit floated past like a balloon. I decided I was alone.

sunday july 1 1979

Older Brother wanted light. We grew still. Pale residue unspooled. If we slept we might dream. How to tell what was dream? At our tent we watched constellations creep through the woods. Now the creek had a surface. Each spirit tried to straighten its one night. A tide of remembrances. What instinct made us touch stones and crayfish and leaves? The smallest beings had the mother inside them. Every thought every action started as feeling in the body, even our town was first a lump of concern. Now we saw town upon town, in unison. It was like reaching page 100 in a transparent book. Older Brother lay down in the tent. I sat at the entrance watching the tide. It wasn't god, but what god comes from, the source, the mother. I told Older Brother and he said *Everything comes from nothing.* The whole woods sang now. Next would be morning and we were inside a mouth with its song rushing past. Less shapes flashed as darkness thinned. We shared the sound of water swaying between creek banks. I watched thoughts pass, each had an ancestor, each slid through a cavern into mass and flesh.

kindness

Some spirits dug into time and buried themselves in its wickedness. I wanted kind ghosts, the comfort of darkness a blanket, a mothering, but some spirits lived further than kindness, in the mother beyond who roils in the night, creation force better than kindness, who makes a creek, who makes every living thing and lets it be, an impulse of making deeper than joy, beyond joy, joy is primitive. Sounds of morning began to throb, a machine here and there, a death to figure out when all seemed alive. In our tongues we felt the notch from our masters. We knew we were in a dream, we knew the dream didn't speak from one direction. Maybe birds didn't notice. One bird called out that it was the world. The question was how to become the dreamer; that's why we were finders, become the dreamer and know the future. We thought we couldn't look just anywhere but we were wrong. Even in birds. Even in each other. We could listen and hear it. We could close our eyes.

church

It was bells. Did we know if we'd slept? Our tent had changed color. Daylight hummed the valley and bells rang over the hum, calling every form to gather. A bell would never eat us. Another deer stepped forward and twitched. Our ears were prehistoric. The woods alighted. I saw the red outline of a rabbit. The question of time grew on us like a scab. I had little dreams as I listened, little dreams as I walked. I dreamt the first encyclopedia was an ear of corn. I dreamt my skin had grown loose and I tried not to walk out of it. When we heard bells we knew to leave. Older Brother looked at his dead walkie-talkie. He said *Was that you last night?* A bell rang what happened, it wore a path in our weightless bodies. Our town sounded real. As we walked up the hill toward its roads we assumed the empty shape of the bell. The tent body between us, our provisions in a sack. I wanted to turn and wave at myself but didn't. The creek would be glowing now. We left our teeth on the ledge because who is whole in this deep weight. We walked out of it.

IV. response

I am losing my because. In the pines.

—Alice Notley

newness

A creek could disappear. Cold on your feet, the shock that someone could love you, then mud. A creek could change direction, time could erase us. Every place housed spirits and some spirits merged and even some spirits had spirits. Parts of us lived in other beings, or the reverse; at dinnertime rooms grew uneven and smaller, Older Brother and I walked through town, listing its newness. Tragic barn stories, teeth in dreams, cars bursting into flame. At the park someone said *They're rich they have a pool table.* An empty van trembled in front of the liquor store. A neighborhood girl told her doll *I'm going to make you think about death.* We walked to the corn-edged rim. Our town had grown shabby in the night. The new god was green, the next people translucent. Older Brother and I threw rocks into the corn. One rock loosened a blue balloon, or turned into a balloon when it entered the corn, or was of course a spirit. We watched it ride over land. There was nowhere to go and no way to turn back. No one explained how to be a boy. The sudden sharp crack of intellectual life would hurt us. I felt Invisible Daughter's cold hand or another hand grew. The problem was time.

sleep

Somewhere in time winter hovered, lonely and romantic, but now summer grew ripe and made us real, awakened to the pagan charge of boyhood, scrotums like alien plant life, midnight erections uncontrollable and strange, transmissions from a land of perverse ghosts, the ruin of a good story. Why do we learn the names of countries? What is dancing? Now we knew sleep itself was a spirit and gave birth, we loped through its crust in morning light. How to have calm legs? The streets were just coffins, really. Hypnosis, the same buildings around and around, only dreams could be touched and passed through and touched us in return. Evidence shone deep in our bodies. We wondered what ghosts thought or were our thoughts ghosts. Sleep fractured, the tumble of the creek swept us, possessed us. Fat Dewey kept asking. We told our parents *It was fun*. We felt the minds of crows shift as we walked. Maybe spirits replaced our sleep with deep ringing, a melted doorway. Maybe after sleep I would be taller, maybe I would know dream from dream.

room

We slept until noon, we rose and said goodbye to old voices of Sunday school teachers, the grocer, the butcher, the jolly crosswalk guard, those who told one story of one god who painted lines and of people who followed, blind, unfound, wanderers in a narrow chute toward heaven, scripted actors reciting to a lost time. We rose and walked the twelve blocks, crouched behind the two bars, picked up bottle caps and learned to flick them like assassins. Now we wanted girls on bicycles. We rose again and shuffled through vacant lots, looking down, we were still finders. Our rooms paled, sank away, rooms of bone quiet shaped like miles apart on the telephone, rooms of magnets. We would probably accelerate now. Something had fallen on the surface of the future, just above us, darkening. I didn't know what to find. Sheets of paper brought on dementia. Each street led its trail of daylight through us. The creek talked crazy and always beneath our thoughts, I couldn't hear it but I could feel what it was like to hear it. There existed no room to enter, no door to close for protection against spirits in the mind. Maybe a mother put her hand in the creek and a child came out. Maybe a father put his hand in the fire and the child disappeared.

creek

I stood on the bridge at dusk. That creek was a talker. Said a body melts. Said carry me. There was a banker in there. An owl in the creek. A devil in the muddy bottom with crayfish hands. A dusty pickup truck passed and we shared the pale light of our nowhere. That creek wanted us in its family, under the bridge, past the sewage plant, into the river and the next river and the next, around the world. That creek wanted us to be as snakes. We talked to our creek. We fell through our creek. We slept with our heads in the creek, all time in our ears. You can't bite a creek. We knelt in overalls, the creek trying to drown us, get us drunk, float us to the next life. That creek was a teardrop sliding down a devil face. We built a model creek, it washed away, we're still in there, smaller and smaller. Tomorrow we'll either be town kids or animals in plaid shirts. Then we'll drive away and go hollow.

tuesday july 3 1979

We gave up our common lives. We held them in quivering bowls outside the butcher shop. Our heads peeled. Our bodies filled with light again. The town shrank and shrank. No one felt comfortable talking to us. Two girls in tank tops appeared at the post office. They had grown up from blades of grass. Our nowhere, crowded with ragweed and cockleburs, became a stage. We followed the girls around, at a distance. I listened for rustling animals; I tried to hear the moon scrape through daylight. I tracked the sound of a dragging muffler. The two girls looked over their shoulders and laughed. I walked around saying *Thank you*. It got late early. I knew how to make a daughter, but that was it.

attention

If you thought about it too long. If fields steamed and sunlight hit the fender, if you rode in the bed of the pickup. If you thought too much about spirits and people found you strange. If you were a finder. Now we knew the woods wandered at night. Who floated. Who emerged from leaves. What daughter woke from a hand and prayed by the creek's pooling eye. I felt Thought-Eating Man nibbling away. The fathers all waved. We never waved back, kept walking into the corn, balloons released around us. We loved our town but some days everything around it was a devil, holding our future. We talked to invisible girls, waited behind the liquor store with our ten-dollar bill, told our story into an empty jar with swollen voices. First a black swan arrived at Hughes' Pond and some kids threw rocks. Then we heard a pastor's wife was buried beneath the church. Then a possum family moved into the culvert. These events were united in the spirit world. Birds sang briefly and disappeared into the creek. What was an egg. What was a gravel pit. Whose dog ran out snarling and what dream did we remember as we ran screaming down the road.

wednesday july 4 1979

We perceived an enemy, outside of town, rising from the golf course. Objects fell from the sky wherever we walked. Not just snow and rain but fire, horses, teeth. A chant fell to our limbs, we tried to shake it out. Cottonwood trees on Goat Island croaked names across the river. Older Brother said he would play a saxophone someday but I knew he wouldn't. A crooked bank of clouds sang in the north. We sat in Older Brother's yard and watched trampled grass stand back up. In the beginning there was no ocean, look at all the ocean now. Around us next lives made their shapes. I thought I should go back to the woods. Because what deep-eyed night cooked the earth. A cricket song entered my left leg. The enemy would fry us under hairy lamps. I should go back and dream the father's dream or throw bread into the creek. Older Brother looked flat into the sky and said *Hurry up.* The enemy's thin horn hovered. I said *Into the earth, sweet thing* to a beetle. Each stone truly had thoughts. Each hour of light made doorways. Each rain shower remembered us and our names were only names of those moments. Fireworks exploded in the starred air above me. I was their child too.

girls

In our town girls appeared suddenly, maybe they were spirits. Diane and Rene let us hold their hands for a time. We hoped our blue eyes haunted them. The playground fell to pieces, eaten by its slow god. We began to "hang out" by "back doors." It didn't involve talking. Did we think enough? The girls told us never to kill toads, toads were someone's children. We walked by the river so dark, we hummed together the properties of time. Spirits roamed in brown light, there were two haunted buildings, snakes and turtles lived on Goat Island. A dog chose where to lie down. We watched cottonwood trees release seeds. The green barbershop upholstery, the rusted cars behind the liquor store. We saw where to hide a magazine. Four hundred and seventy-nine people dreamt our town. Days rushed toward us. Diane and Rene walked as daughters in mangled light. We stood ramshackle and swaying on the bridge and looked into the woods. A leaf shone. I remembered a hoofbeat. Earth language had crept into us. Did we imagine we had walked through the woods? A cold tongue traveled the ground. The woods had walked through us. Diane and Rene shied from our sidelooks. They laughed at us. Older Brother told them *We saw vapors.*

historical

Our town made itself into dream. Ripped up sidewalks and put down boardwalks; installed hitching posts for horses from the 1800s. It began to celebrate the lowly marigold. It raised a clean ghost. Packs of bikers blew through, evaporating us in their wake. Limestone walls spoke in a sea language. Someone gave the daughter a terrible flower. Our town took a wooden shed and made a covered bridge to Goat Island. The old stagecoach road, the brewery, the pony express: ruins resurfaced as the outline to a great reverie. Light arrived in other light, alive. What was beneath the church, or who. We could make our town duel time. Invent it. Older Brother wanted a girlfriend and a future. Our sky kept close as an eggshell. Maps pleased us by doing nothing, by not showing where spirits released their troubles. We found the types of light alive in woods, said they too were nameless. Our town lived twice. Trees blossomed then fruit made the blossoms go blind. Tourists would come, spilled from legendary buckets onto our earth. Historians would ring the bells but in the woods history meant nothing.

kiss

Where we kissed Diane, first one then the other, it was a contest, her hair caught on the rough brick of the post office, each brick alive. What was in the water, what surfaced. Where men in glass caves made twilight, someone chose you through a sea of human noise, walked by your house in summer, found out when practice ended, chose you by red thoughts in an unknown space of mind, someone unknown thought of you in the dark and you were unbelievably chosen to be kissed. Maybe someone said a prayer for the safe arrival of shy people through dangerous mountains, then the touch of kiss and from its spark I saw a future ghost in Diane's hair waiting to be born, heard the words it used to bear flesh. The other world could be anywhere, maybe the first person who died invented it. Our town seemed a mirage, a decrepit butterfly floating through the land of the dead. The kiss developed in caves and found its way to our faces. A tractor sounded from near fields, reached us and tried to strangle our kiss. Crayfish could be simple spirits. Was this the blue garden? Were we unknowing magicians? Older Brother stood watching us. I forgot life on earth.

saturday july 7 1979

I went alone if that was still possible. From the ditch again, along the creek, I walked the woods but didn't know it as woods. I saw the father walking ahead, saw clouds thrown at the ordinary town. Of course the stars were gods. Beds of flattened grasses where deer had dreamt. He paused along the ridge to find what he might never find and went on. I knew we had already walked through a sleeping mother or death. A palace of guts. I saw small lights in the creek below, just starlight, just moonlight and the father walked through his time. I heard a cow or faraway ghost or spirit or stomach. I wanted to creep near, the moon dearly full of us. I wanted to carry him in a jar. Creek light sparkled his hypnotized face. Three clouds and one moon. I saw Thought-Eating Man flicker, just the father's shadow now. I saw their path. I hoped to follow but feared to get lost. The woods already owned me. The father got bluer and turned again to face me. The woods blued too and howled along, the father walked at me past bleak gaping mouths of trees. Another creek appeared. I saw his transparent fingernails. The moon grew. He looked at footsteps, he sought me. The father so close I trembled. Each leaf warbled. Then the father walked through me, I turned, there was no one. The father walked through me and disappeared. What now?

dream II

Late in the night I woke and walked again. Our house had changed shape. The hallway reached beyond sight, stretched over the road, impossibly, over town. I passed door after door, mysterious, I tried to be a finder. Each door was one day of my life, horrible door for each day and if I opened a door that's the day my life would start, I would wake into it. I kept walking, in horrible light, in thought of the last door. I knew Invisible Daughter was behind one door and I wanted to find her, I wanted to watch her being born. I put my ear to a pale green door. Behind and in front of me, the hallway of days, rubbery and without rest. Who would build such a thing. Who promises what to a pebble or leaf or boy. When I opened the door I sat up in bed and Invisible Daughter sat next to me. I asked her if I was in the past or the future. She said *Either both or neither.* Her hand cold as the creek. Out the window, the street appeared to flutter. My eye moved like a camera and clicked. I was in my bedroom again, upright, staring at wood-grain faces in the door. I saw a silent bee leave the grain. It flew toward my forehead. As it flew into me, I lost myself and fell into darkness.

name

Morning grew around my bed and I thought of the creek as a rock thinks when it is underwater, as a rock when it is listening. The creek stretched its name beyond lives, kept saying the name, creek that started nowhere. A person outside time could know it. Who lived as long as a creek? Only a god, we supposed. We took fragments of the creek's name as our names and never spoke them; we took on unspeakable names. The creek like the endless number in math class but better it was alive and talked to us and changed shape and kept saying its name and how names we didn't know would be revealed at death, understood at death or when a person stops being a person at that moment our lives would make a song-like sense then vanish. From bed I followed the creek through the homes of women's bodies backward to the first big breath. A rock listened. Morning turned palm light over us. I smelled a pancake. Glass of milk, rescue me. Trees talked daylight and I stepped right in.

path

I had the rest of my days to walk through what, in what footsteps. We were sacrificial food. We didn't know our town happened in a nest of spirits, in the dark, full of noise, our town gray and brown and creeping green, there rolled the blue river, there nests grew purple in trees. Our town made of house, house, haunted house, post office, liquor store, opera hall, barbershop, bank, gas station, house, house, park, trees, swingset, river, dam, bridge, sewage plant, campground, creek, sledding hill, old brewery, log cabin, trailer court, baseball field, school, house, house, courthouse, pile of leaves, noise, ghost, shed, garage, flowerbed, horse. Older Brother lived two blocks east with his parents. I lived two blocks west with mine. We smelled river from our upper rooms. Fat Dewey always drunk and his dog barked all night. Candy wrappers flew around. Older Brother's backyard sloped down to the creek and owls lived there and called to us. Our parents called back, they made a map of the wind and put our names on a current so the map drifted through our heads. Trees were maps of water and spirits read them. We said *When you die you know your name* and out came the future, and what could I see.

love

I found myself alone in the woods and very tired. I lay down beneath an oak tree. Another forest appeared, breathing and thick, another forest grew out of my head, one dream hibernated and one dream was sent into the father. I found myself alone in the woods. Ancestors passed into me and pulled, our sounds spread unto the sky. We walked in light from what flesh, dragged by what clouds. Our town slid down its dead god's belly. I wanted to know all the bells and all they meant. Once Invisible Daughter held my hand along the ridge, once she waited somewhere blue, suddenly cold. What walked ahead on the blinding path? I loved Invisible Daughter. I loved our spell along the ridge. We knew civilization would always be a failure. But I love her today, that's all I remember. At the end of summer the creek smoothed to a stop. I looked down at my reflection. My plain face, the dim sky, our dream. The terrible flower, it never opened. I saw how I would betray her and I didn't want to be a boy anymore. But time traps everyone in unknown light. We found our jobs, we kept moving. Unto the sky. Am I a spirit now, telling this? If you know, say it to me.

Photo by Sarah Fox

John Colburn is originally from Mantorville, MN, and is an editor and co-publisher for Spout Press. His poetry chapbook *Kissing* was published by Fuori Editions in 2002. A second chapbook, *The Lawrence Welk Diaries*, appeared from WinteRed Press in 2006. He lives in Minneapolis. With his wife, the poet Sarah Fox, he tends The Center for Visionary Poetics. He is also a member of the improvised music collective Astronaut Cooper's Parade.

CPSIA information can be obtained at www.ICGtesting.com
Printed in the USA
LVOW080520050413

327751LV00004B/187/P